GW01281015

I'd like to dedicate this book to my grandma, Rhoda Ducharme Hayward,
for encouraging me to be who I am and for letting me roam around
in nature and in my imagination.
—P.P.

"Autumn" originally appeared in *The Poems of Alexander Lawrence Posey*, ed. Minnie H. Posey (Topeka, KS: Crane & Co., 1910).

Backmatter © 2024 ABRAMS
Illustrations © 2024 Paige Pettibon

Book design by Melissa Nelson Greenberg
These images were created using the procreate program with marker and graphite digital brushes.

Published in 2024 by Cameron Kids, an imprint of ABRAMS. All rights reserved. No portion of this book may be reproduced, stored in a retrieval system, or transmitted in any form or by any means, mechanical, electronic, photocopying, recording, or otherwise, without written permission from the publisher.

Library of Congress Control Number: 2023947380
ISBN: 978-1-949480-58-0

Printed in China

10 9 8 7 6 5 4 3 2 1

Cameron Kids books are available at special discounts when purchased in quantity for premiums and promotions as well as fundraising or educational use. Special editions can also be created to specifications.
For details, contact specialsales@abramsbooks.com or the address below.

ABRAMS The Art of Books
195 Broadway, New York, NY 10007
abramsbooks.com

petite poems

AUTUMN

by ALEXANDER POSEY

illustrated by
PAIGE PETTIBON

cameron kids

In the dreamy silence
Of the afternoon,

A cloth of gold is woven
Over wood and prairie;

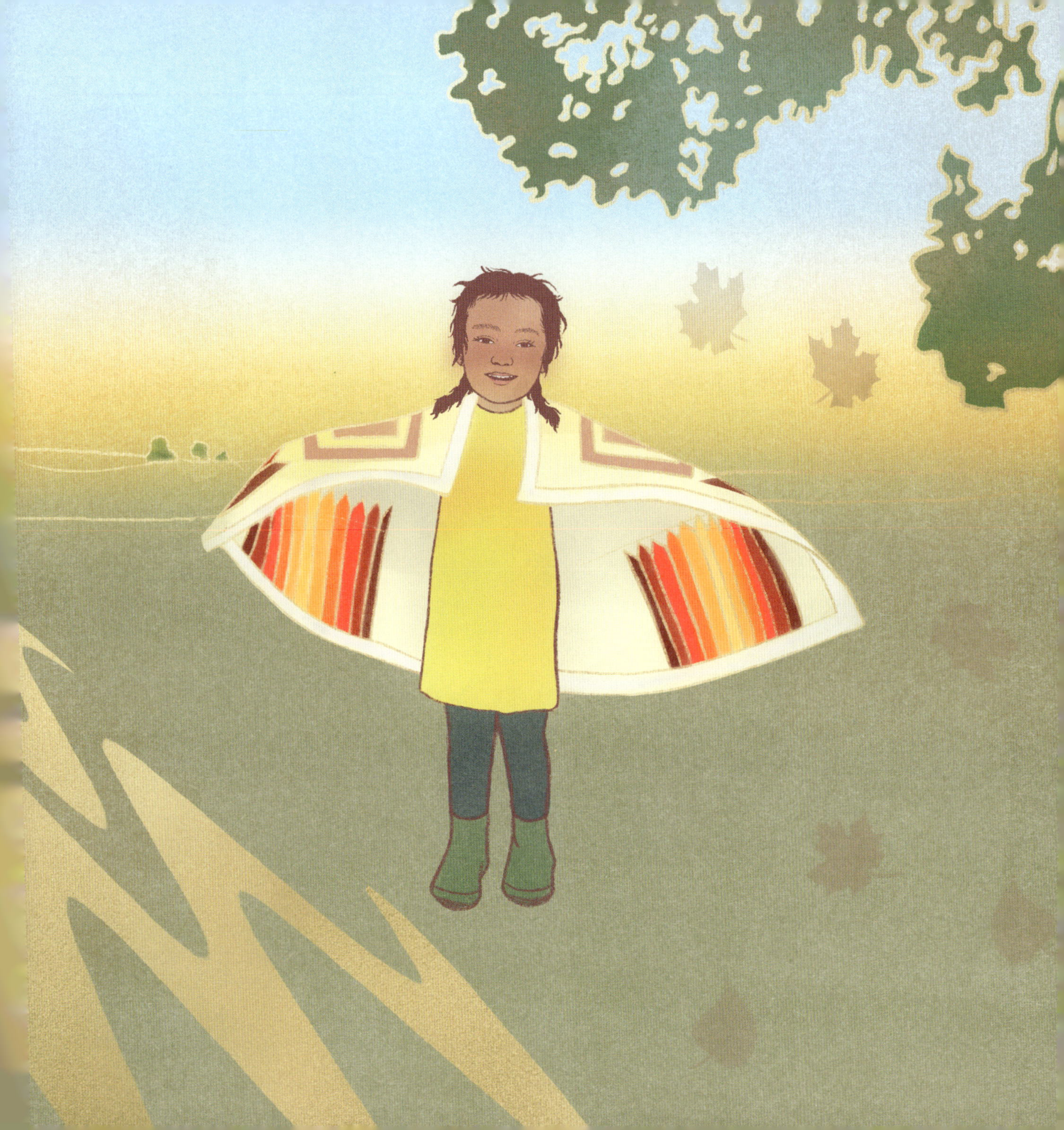

And the jaybird, newly
Fallen from the heaven,
Scatters cordial greetings,

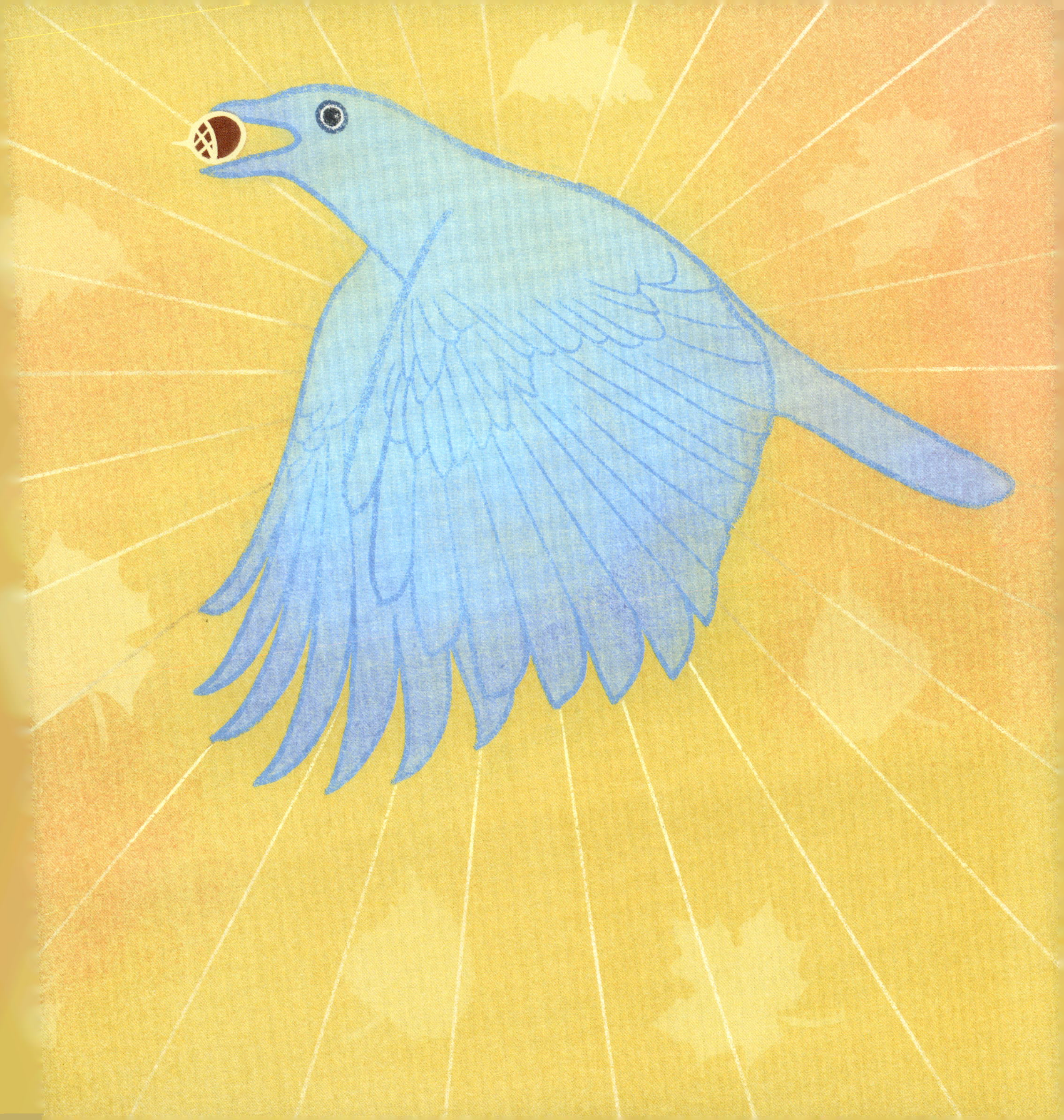

And the air is filled with
Scarlet leaves, that, dropping,

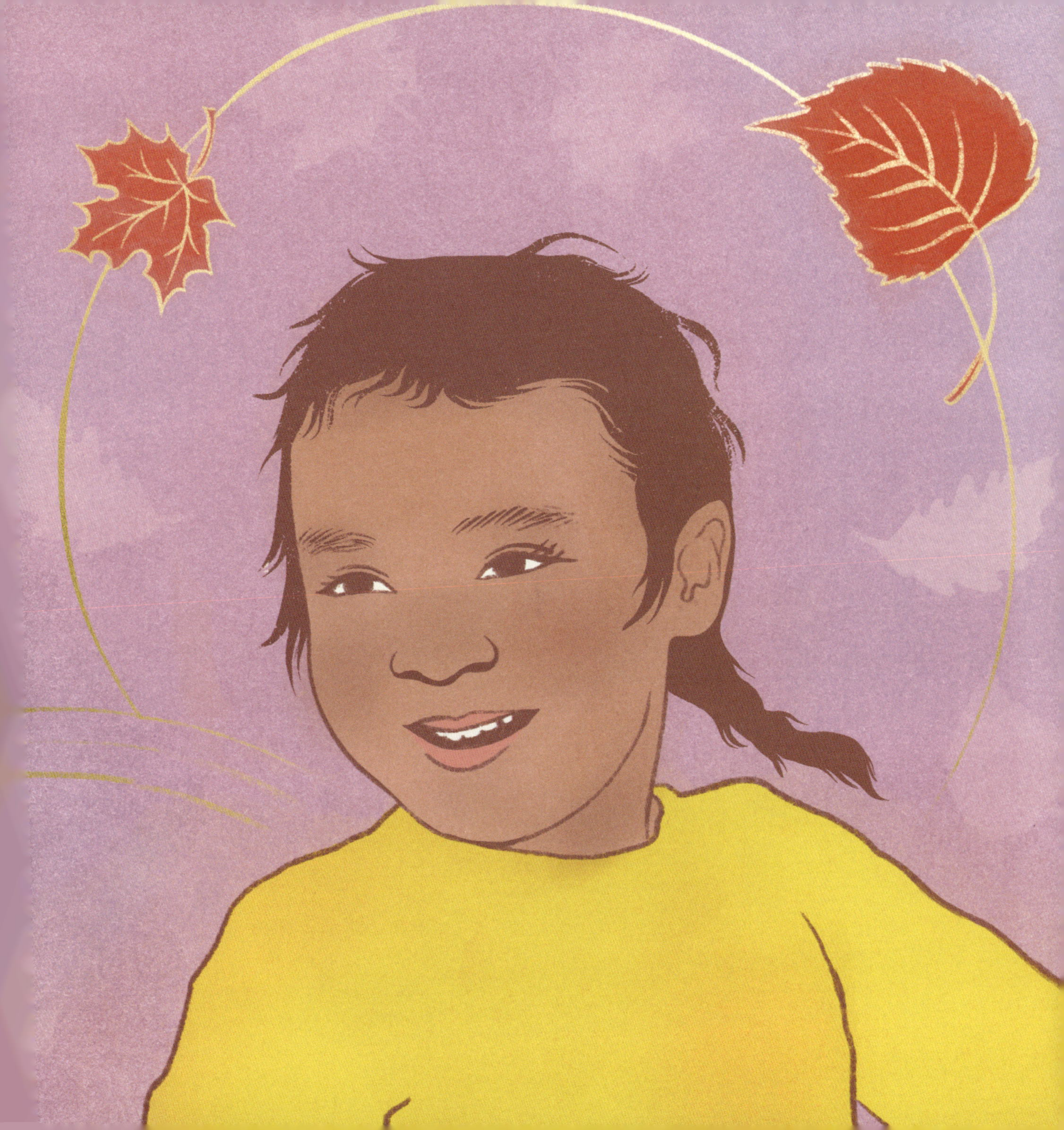

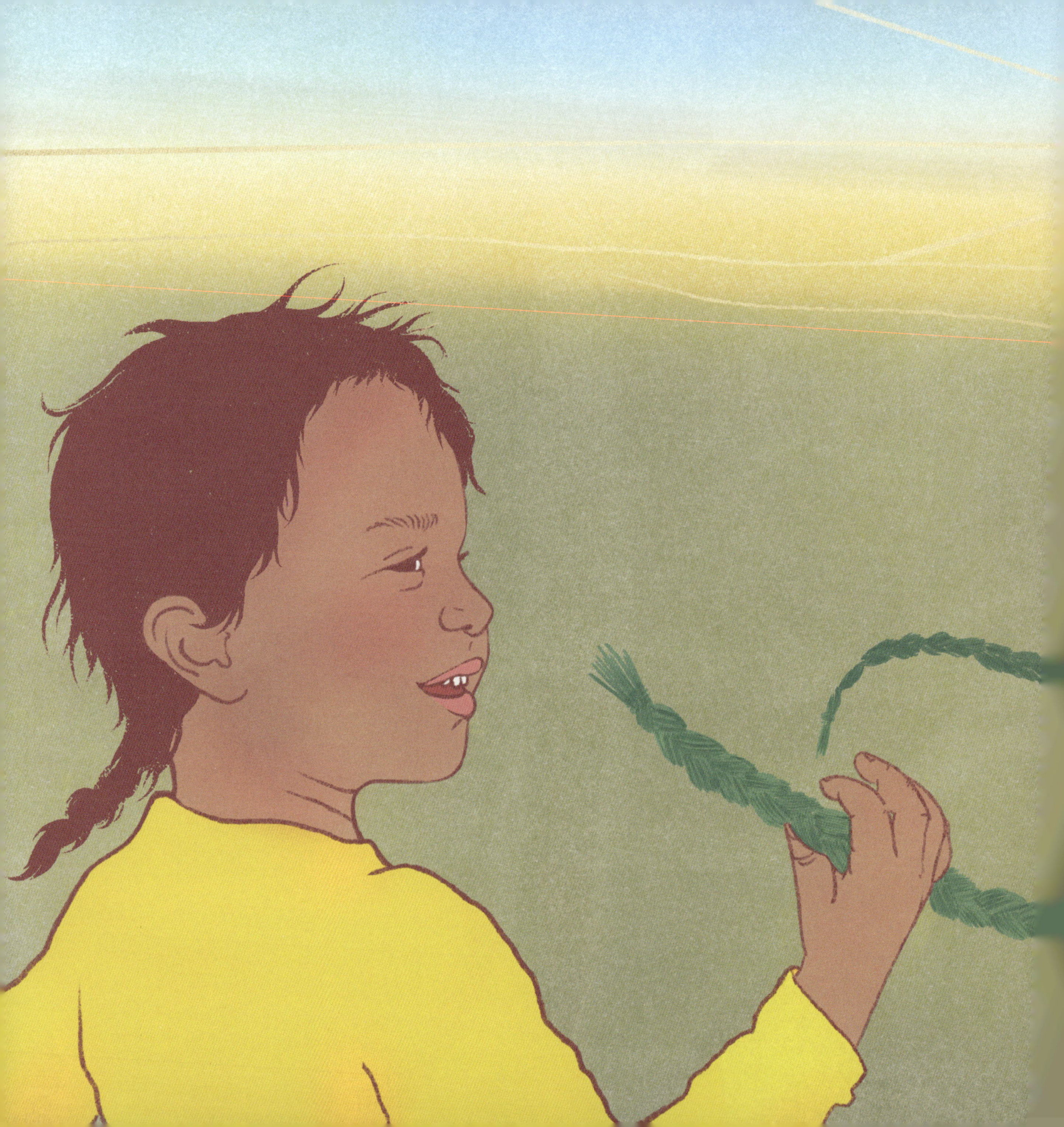

Rise again, as ever,
With a useless sigh for

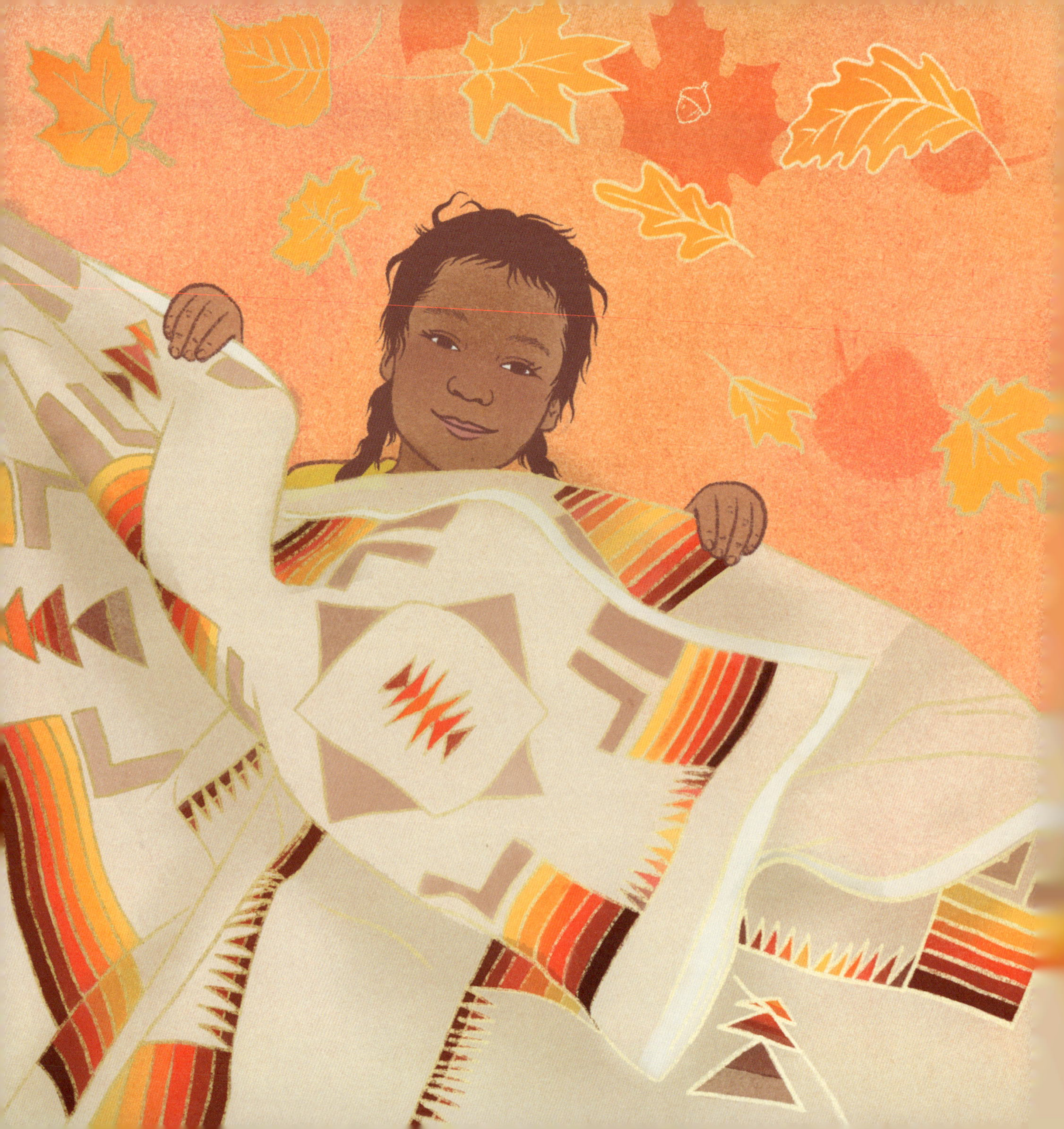

Rest

—and it is Autumn.

AUTUMN

by ALEXANDER POSEY

In the dreamy silence
Of the afternoon, a
Cloth of gold is woven
Over wood and prairie;
And the jaybird, newly
Fallen from the heaven,
Scatters cordial greetings,
And the air is filled with
Scarlet leaves, that, dropping,
Rise again, as ever,
With a useless sigh for
Rest—and it is Autumn.

ABOUT THE POEM

"Autumn" depicts a dreamy fall day full of jaybird songs and scarlet leaves dancing through the air. In this poem, Alexander Posey celebrates the changing of the seasons as the golden sun sets on summer and the world prepares for a time of rest.

ABOUT THE POET

Alexander Posey was Muscogee poet, journalist, humorist, and editor. In 1901, he founded the first Indigenous daily newspaper, which gained him national recognition. Alexander lived in an incredibly turbulent time for the Muscogee Nation, and he used his writing to not only criticize the American government's treatment of Indigenous peoples but also to advocate for a majority-Indigenous state. He was a firm believer that Indigenous nations should have the right to govern themselves. His poetry celebrated the history of Indigenous peoples and the beautiful landscapes of his home in modern-day Oklahoma, where the Muscogee Nation was forced to relocate by the US government.

To learn more about Alexander Posey, visit the Academy of American Poets, www.poets.org.

Alexander Posey (1873–1908), courtesy of the Oklahoma Historical Society Research Division

A NOTE FROM THE ILLUSTRATOR

For this beautiful poem, I wanted to highlight our connection with the feeling of transitioning. At the beginning of the book, we sense the end of summer, and by the end, we are fully immersed in fall. My goal was to welcome the gifts nature has to offer us by illuminating how we can use our five senses to take in our surroundings: the smell of harvested sweetgrass, the touch of wind blowing our hair, the sound of birds, the sight of fire-colored leaves, and the taste of a nutty acorn. I hope readers and listeners feel cozy with the crisp air of autumn. Let the protagonist guide you as you take the time to appreciate the precious softness of the season.

THE FEELING OF AUTUMN

"Autumn" is all about the begining of fall. What do you notice about this time of year? What colors are the changing leaves? What flavors does fall bring: a crisp apple, a ripe pumpkin, or something else? Use your five senses to see, hear, touch, tase, and smell what autumn is like where you live. Write a poem or draw a picture about what autumn feels like to you!